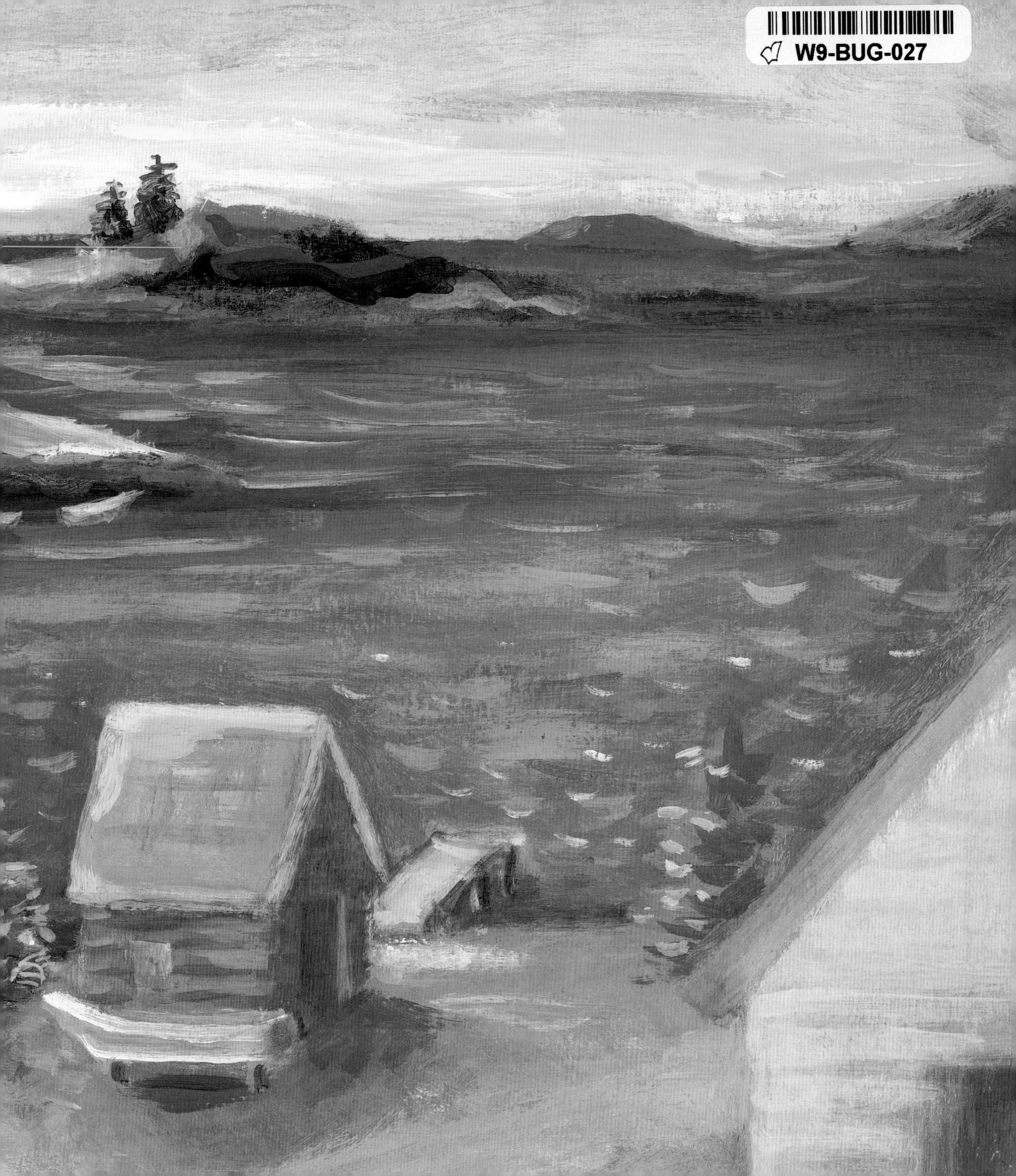

For Mum and Dad, who loaded us into
the station wagon each weekend so we
could explore the wild wonder of
the Maine coast. For Fiona and Enrica,
my fellow tidal-pool explorers.
Heartfelt thanks to Liza, James, Lili,
Richard, Sarah, Jim, Ann, Melanie, Mona,
Walter, and my dear Srini K. for their
kindness and support.
Bless you all.
—C.J.

Text copyright © 1924, 1930 by the President and
Fellows of Harvard College
Illustrations copyright © 2006 by Cynthia Jabar
All rights reserved
Distributed in Canada by Douglas & McIntyre Ltd.
Color separations by Chroma Graphics PTE Ltd.
Printed and bound in the United States of America
by Phoenix Color Corporation
Designed by Barbara Grzeslo
First edition, 2006
1 3 5 7 9 10 8 6 4 2

www.fsgkidsbooks.com

Library of Congress Cataloging-in-Publication Data
Field, Rachel, 1894–1942.
    Grace for an island meal / Rachel Field ;
pictures by Cynthia Jabar.— 1st ed.
      p.   cm.
    ISBN-13: 978-0-374-32759-0
    ISBN-10: 0-374-32759-9
    1. Blessing and cursing—Juvenile poetry.
2. Dinners and dining—Juvenile poetry.
3. Islands—Juvenile poetry.   4. Children's poetry,
American.   I. Jabar, Cynthia, ill.   II. Title.

PS3511.I25G73 2006
811'.54—dc22

                        2004056433

CRANBERRY
ISLES

GRACE *for an* ISLAND MEAL

Rachel Field

Pictures by Cynthia Jabar

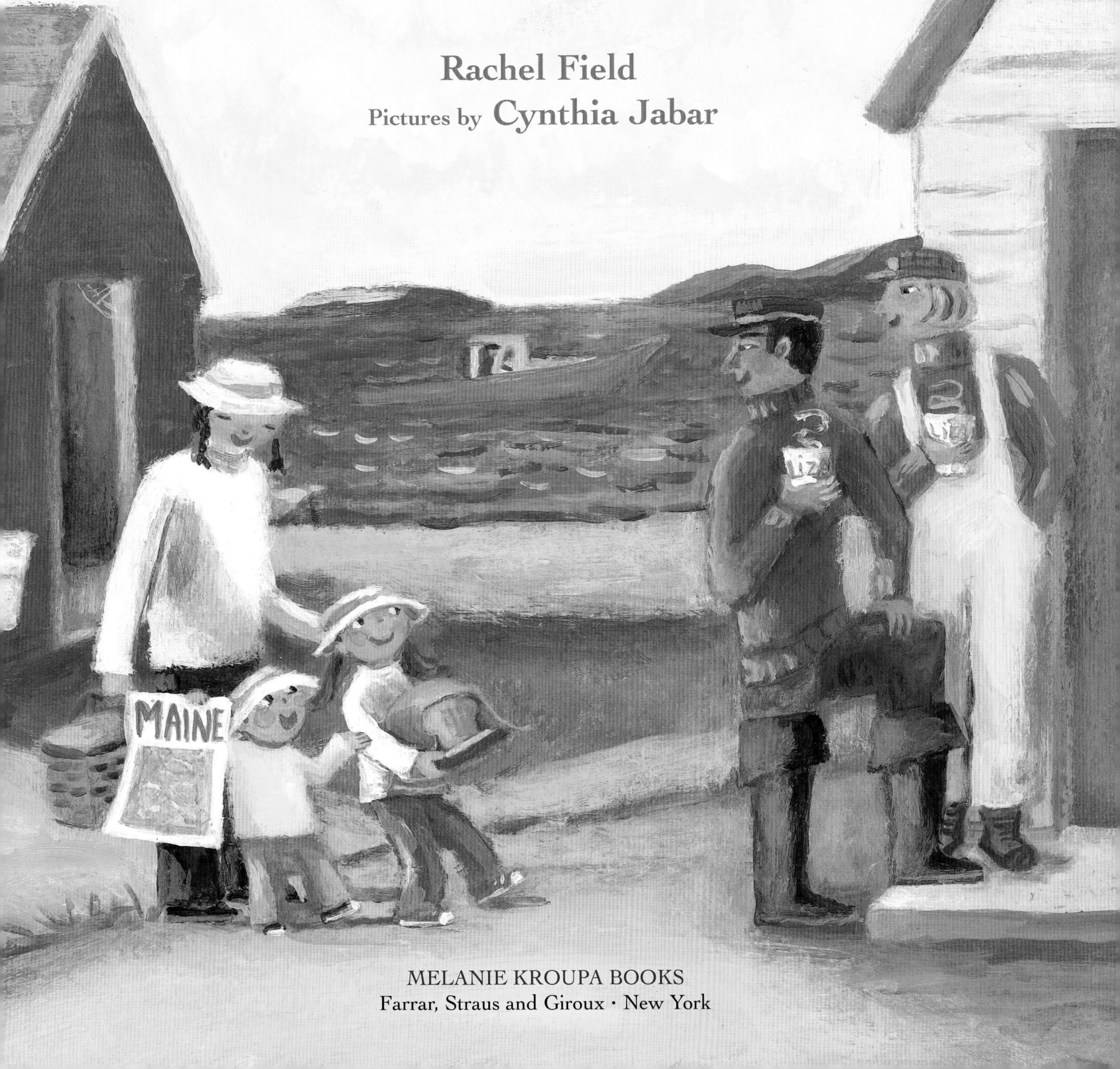
MAINE

MELANIE KROUPA BOOKS

Farrar, Straus and Giroux · New York

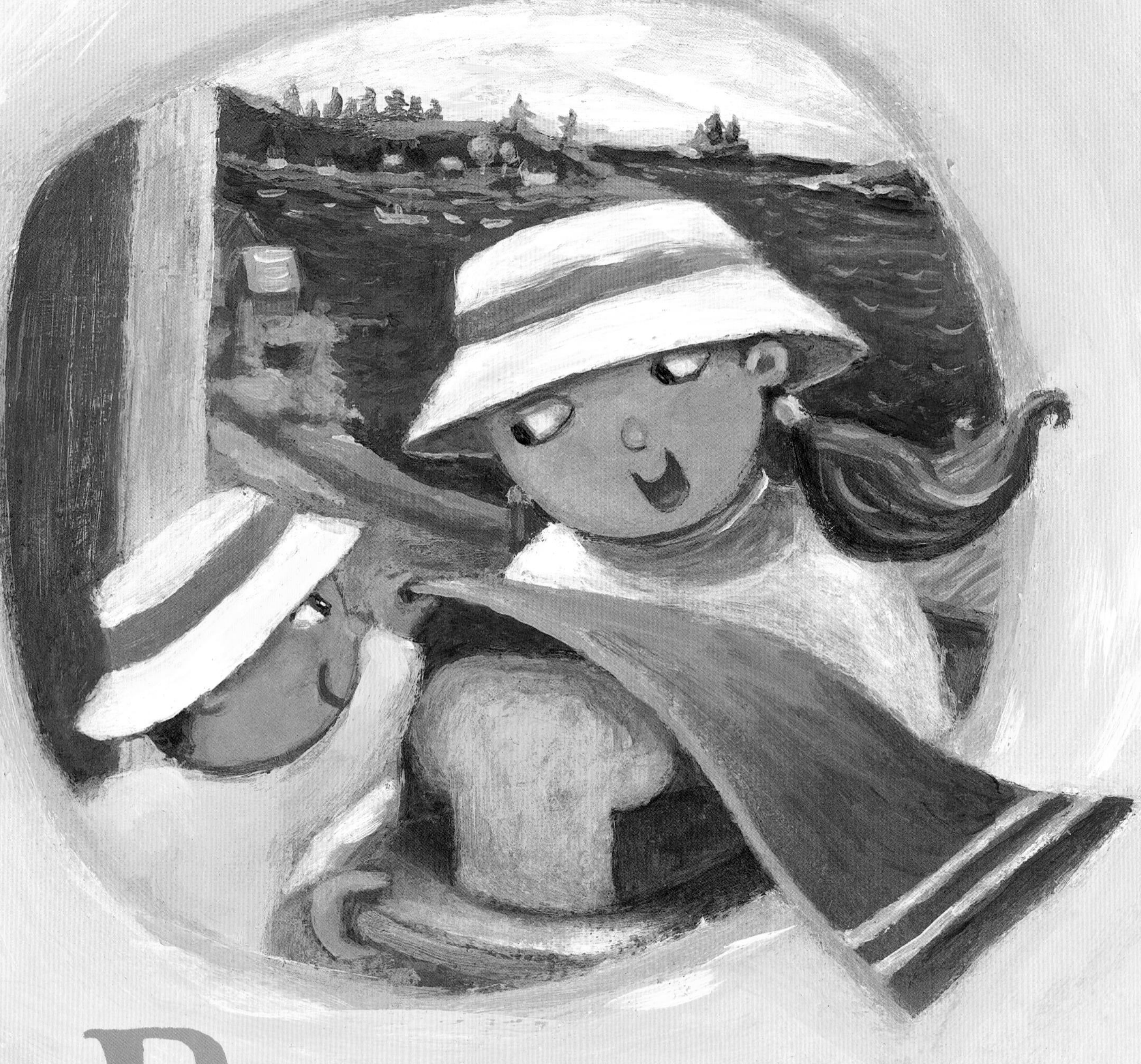

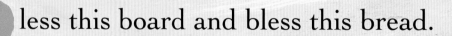

Bless this board and bless this bread.

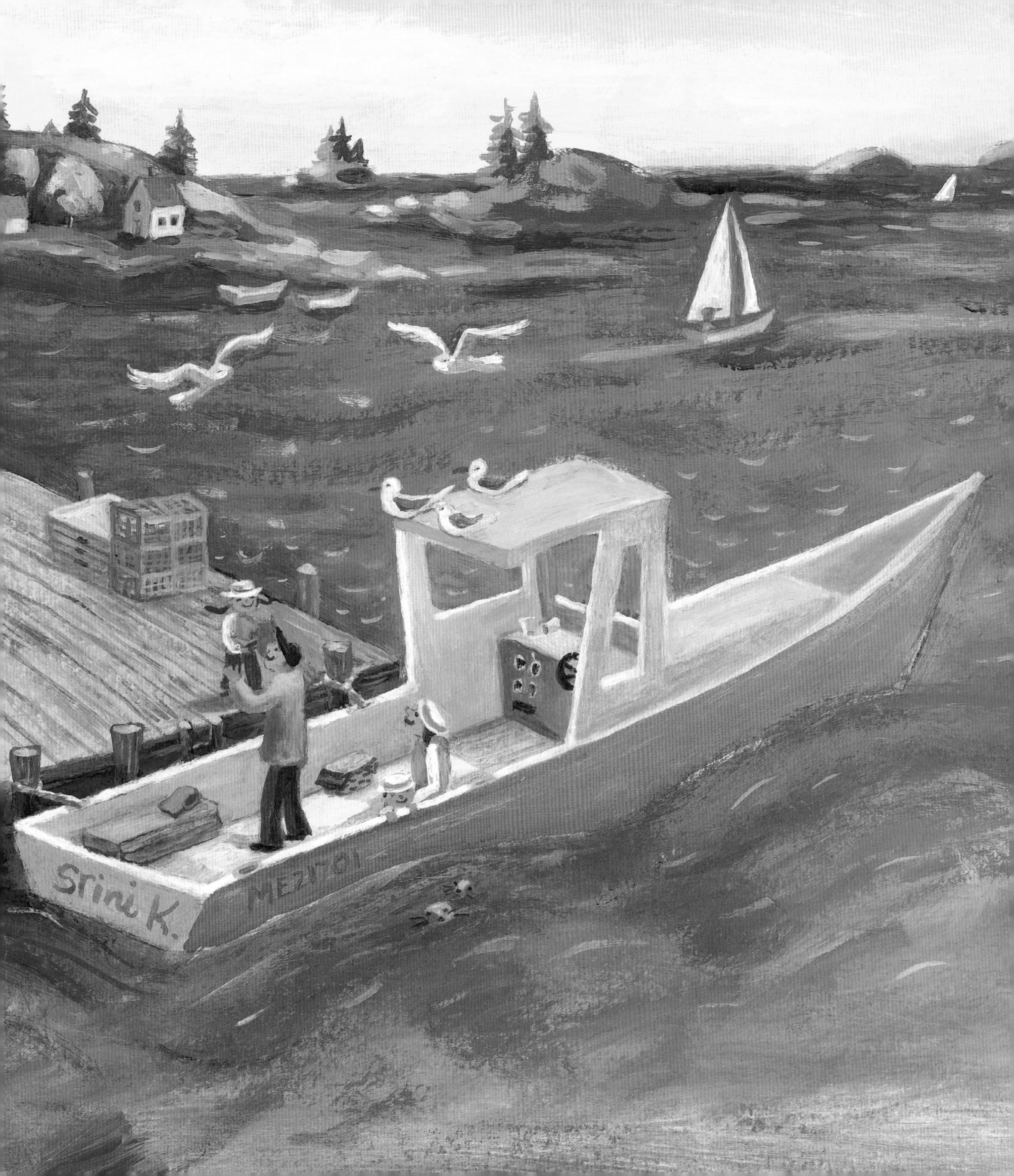
Srini K.
ME2101

Bless this skylight overhead

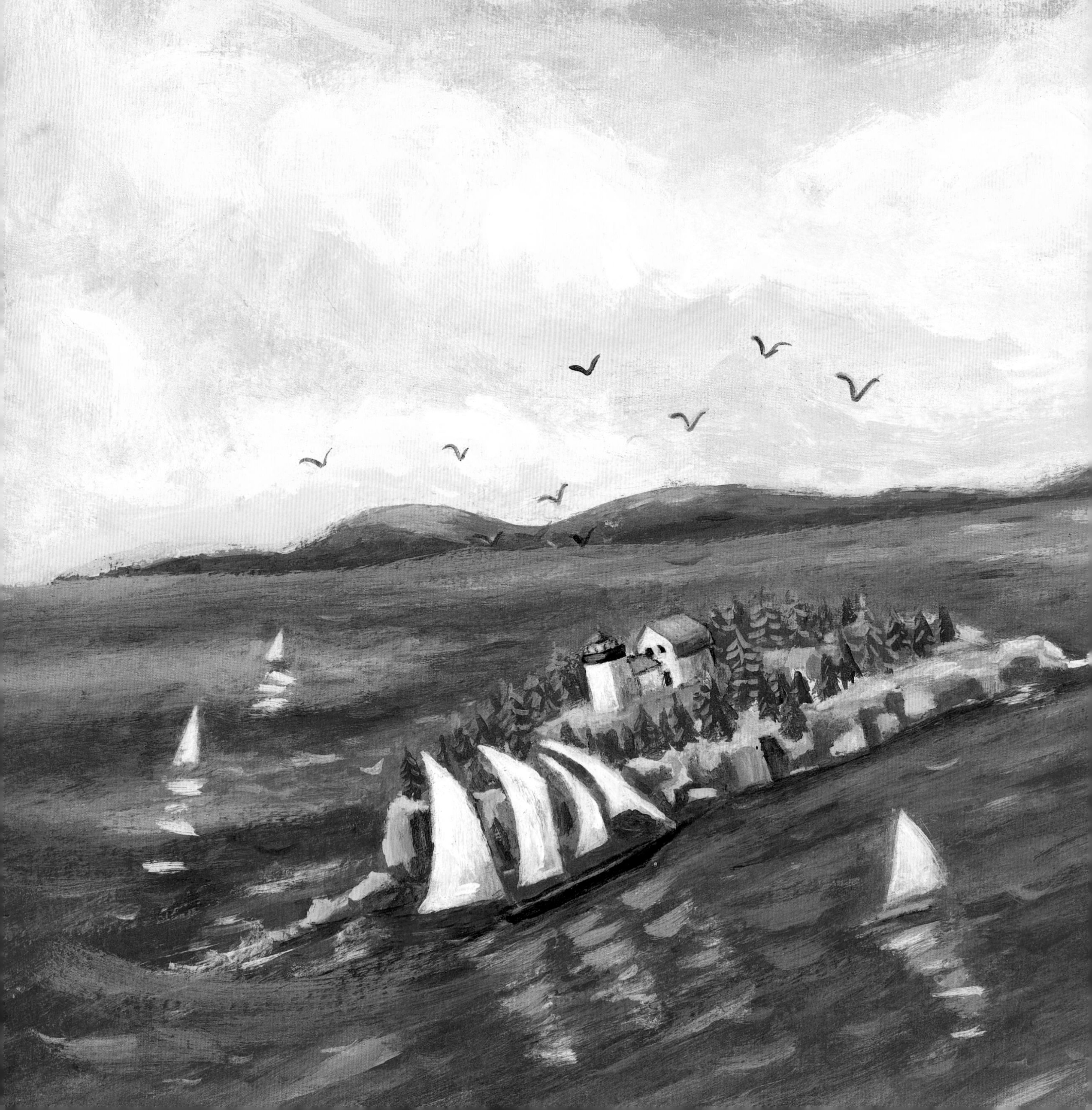

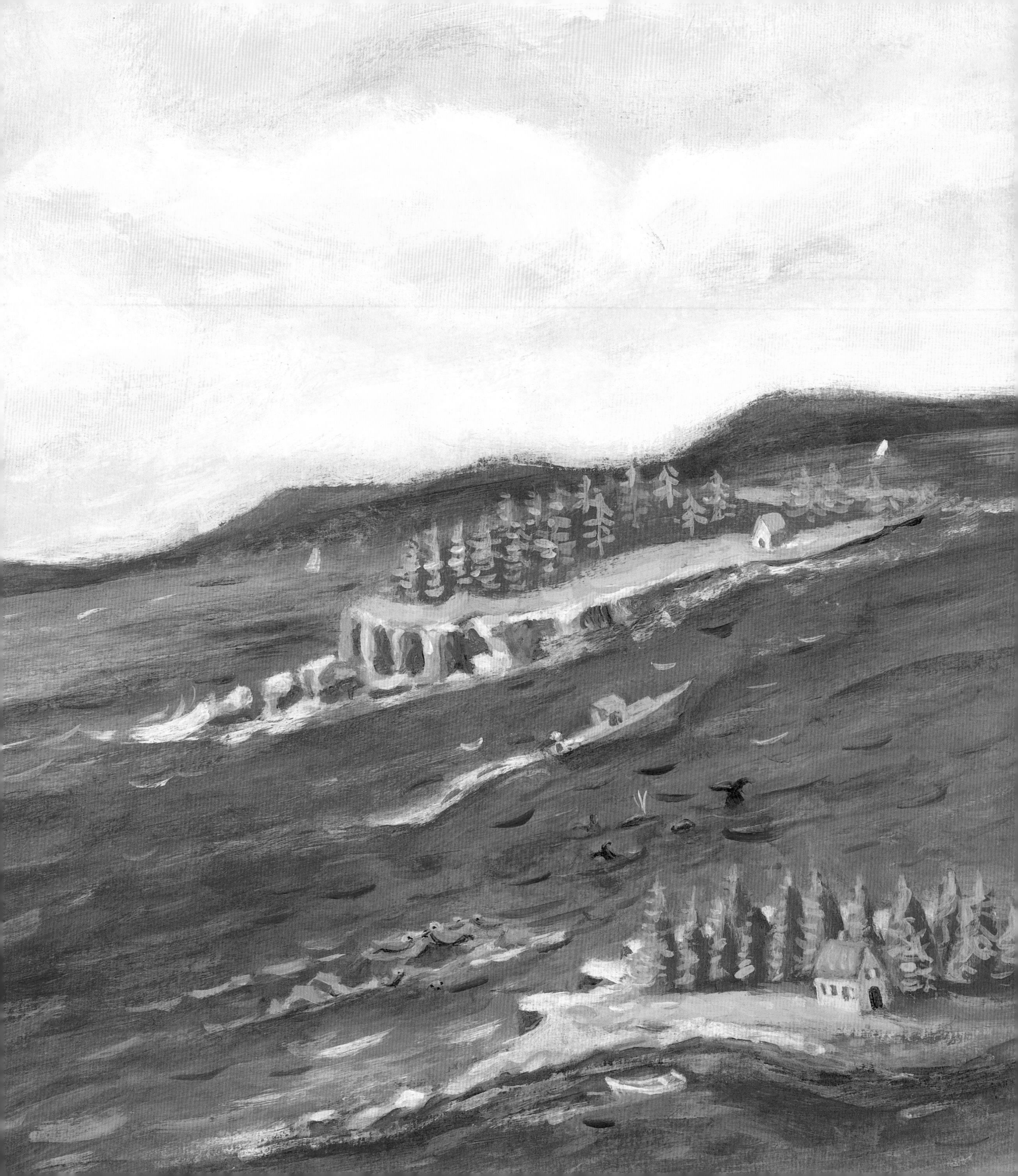

through which any eye may see
wheeling gull and blowing tree.

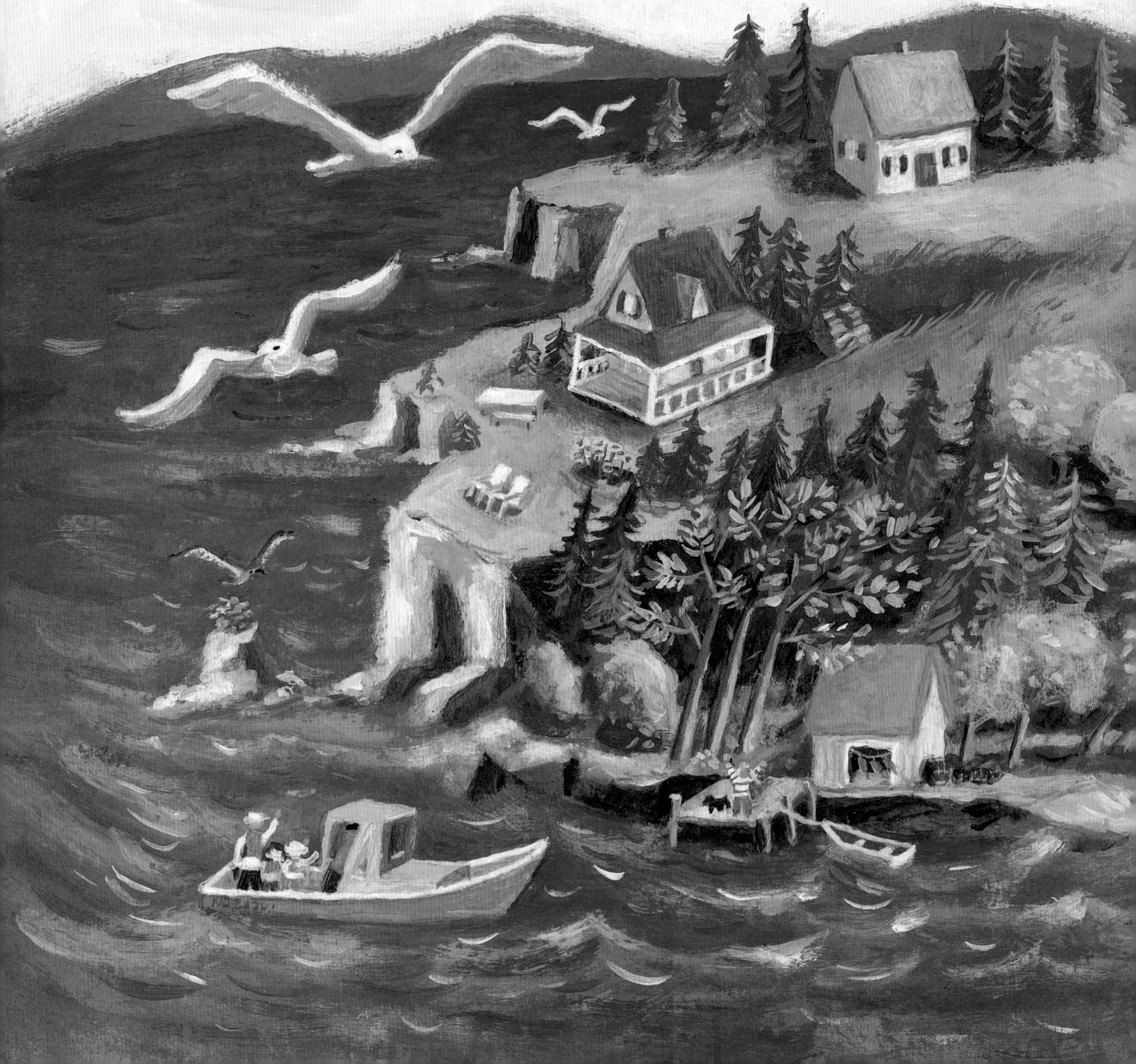

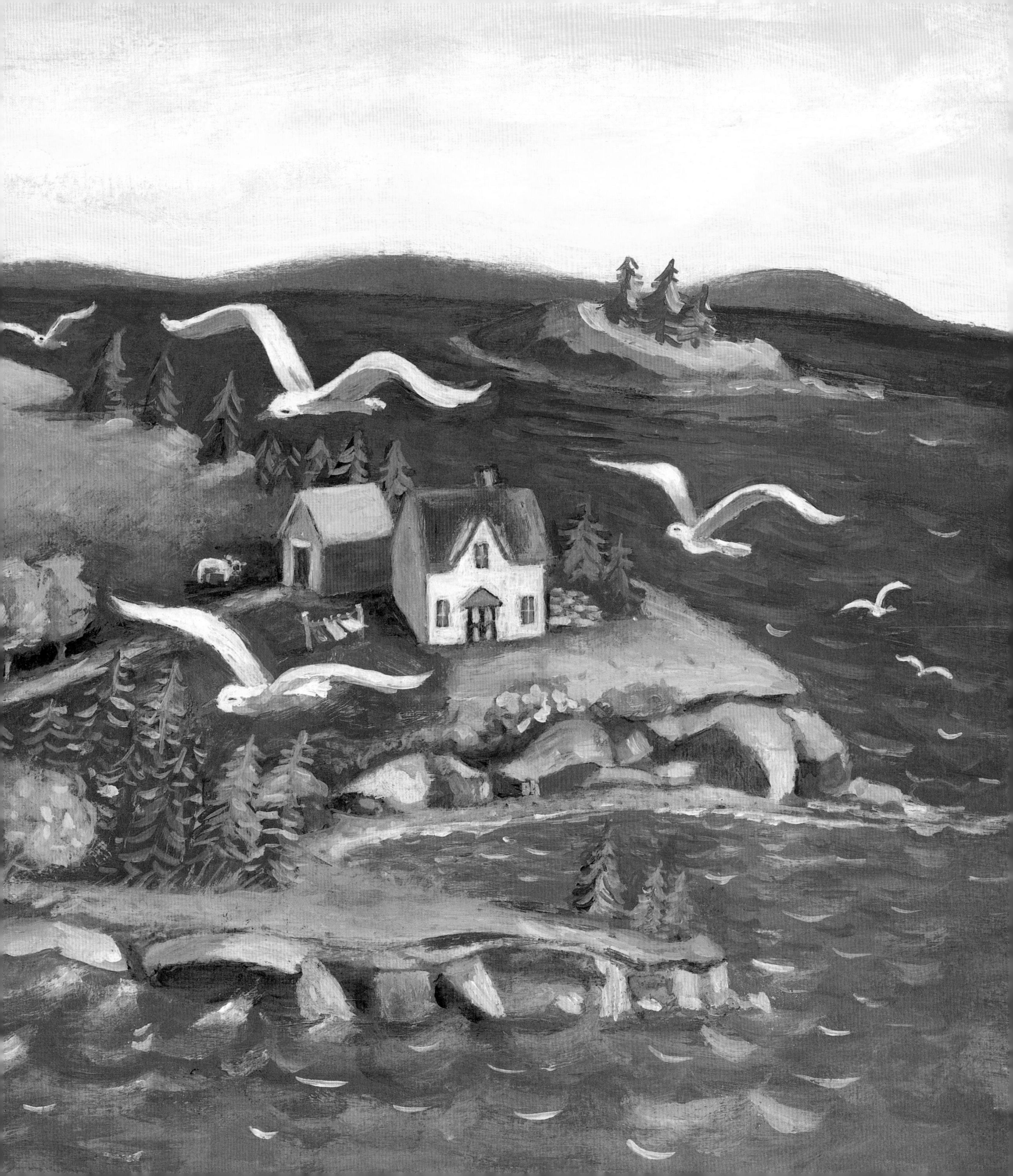

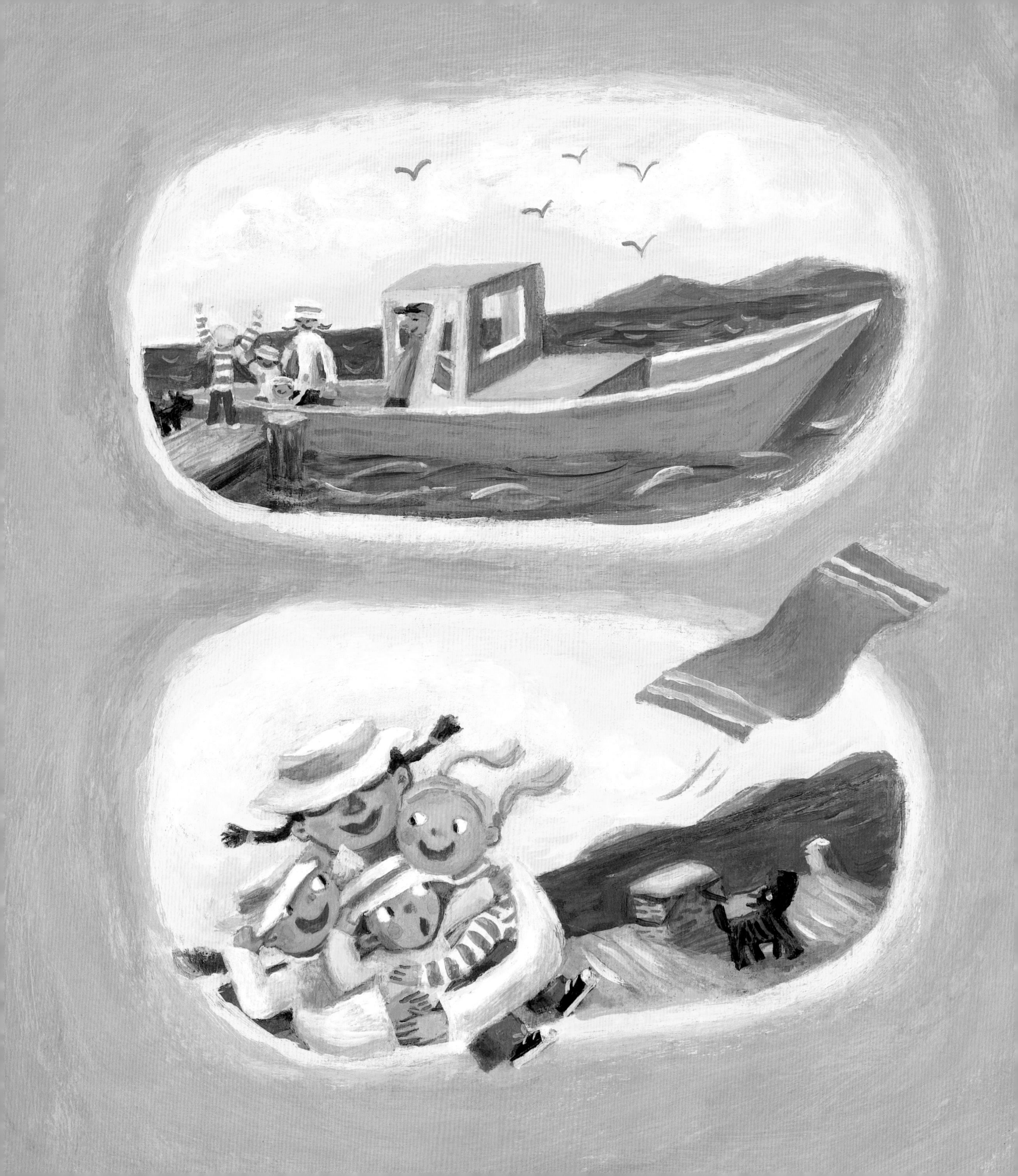

Bless this cloth of woven blue.

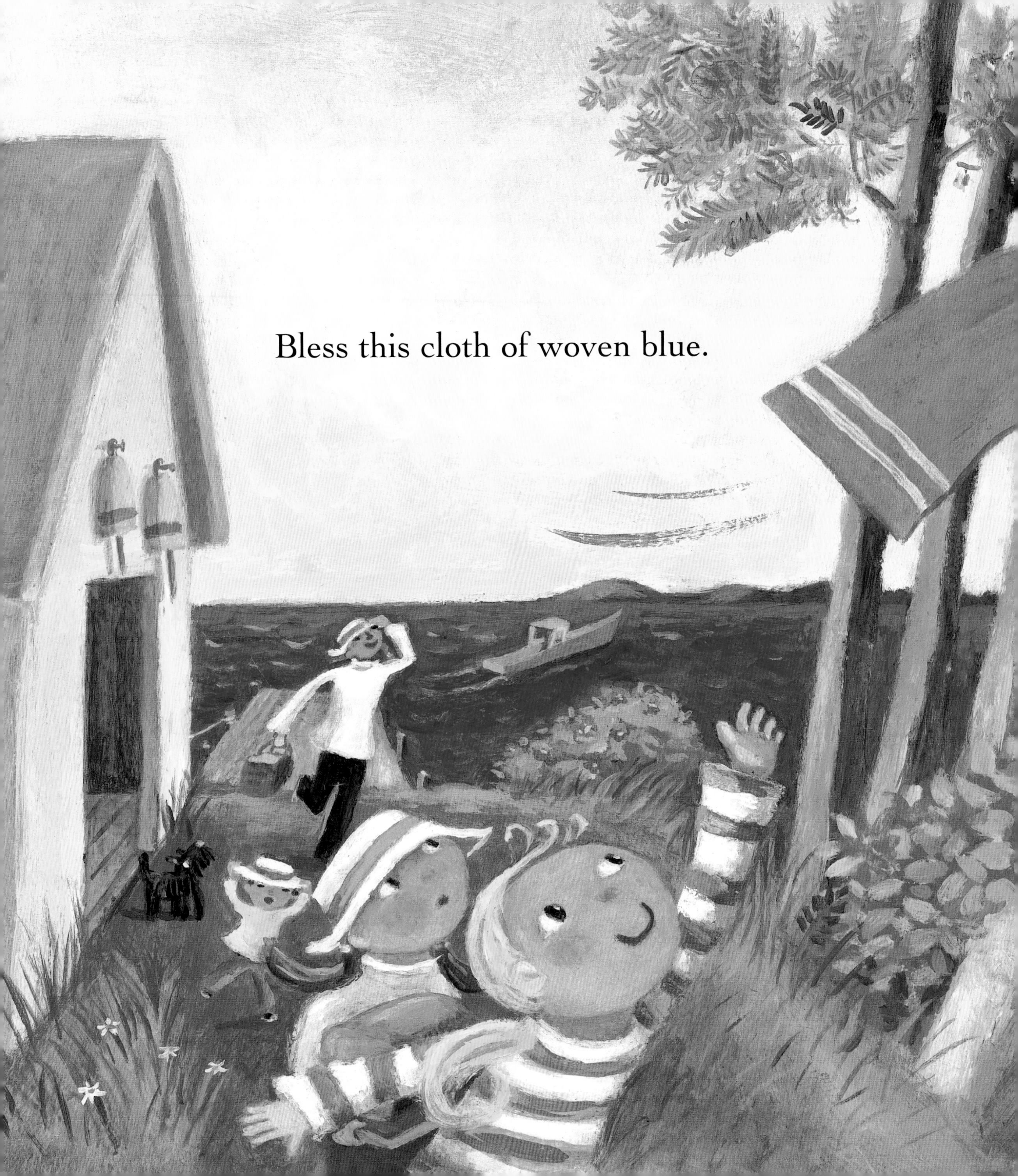

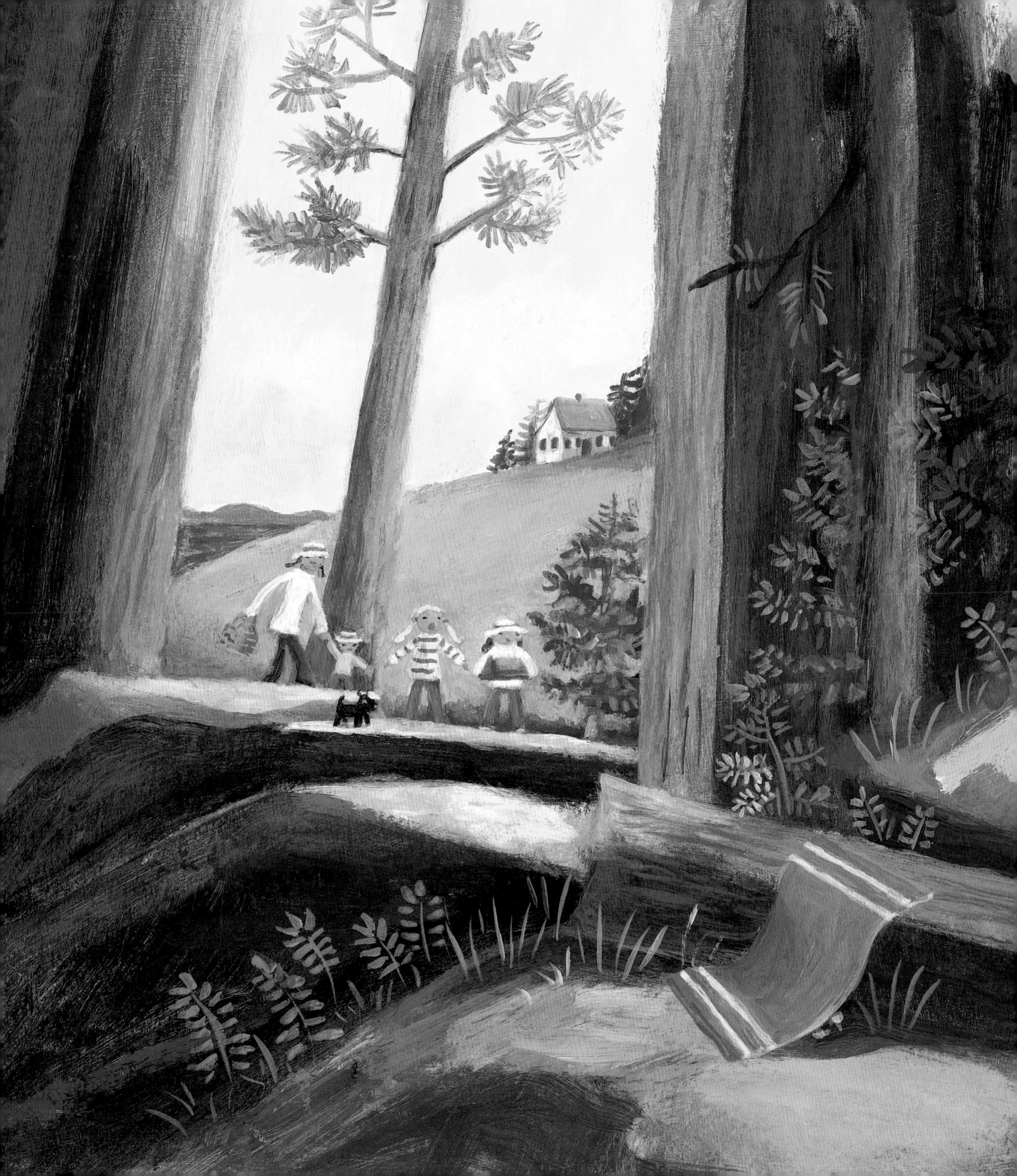

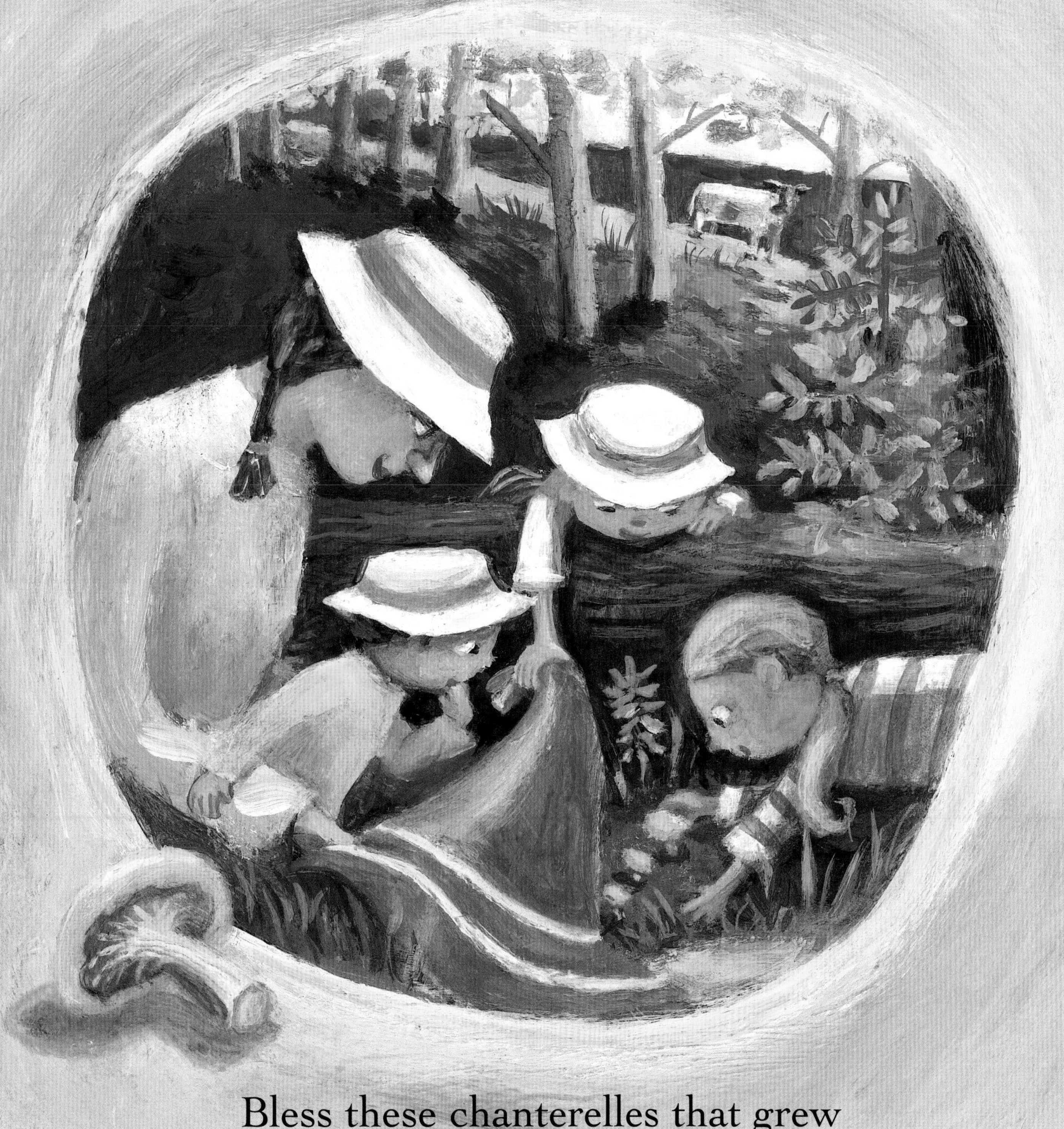

Bless these chanterelles that grew
in secret under mossy bough.

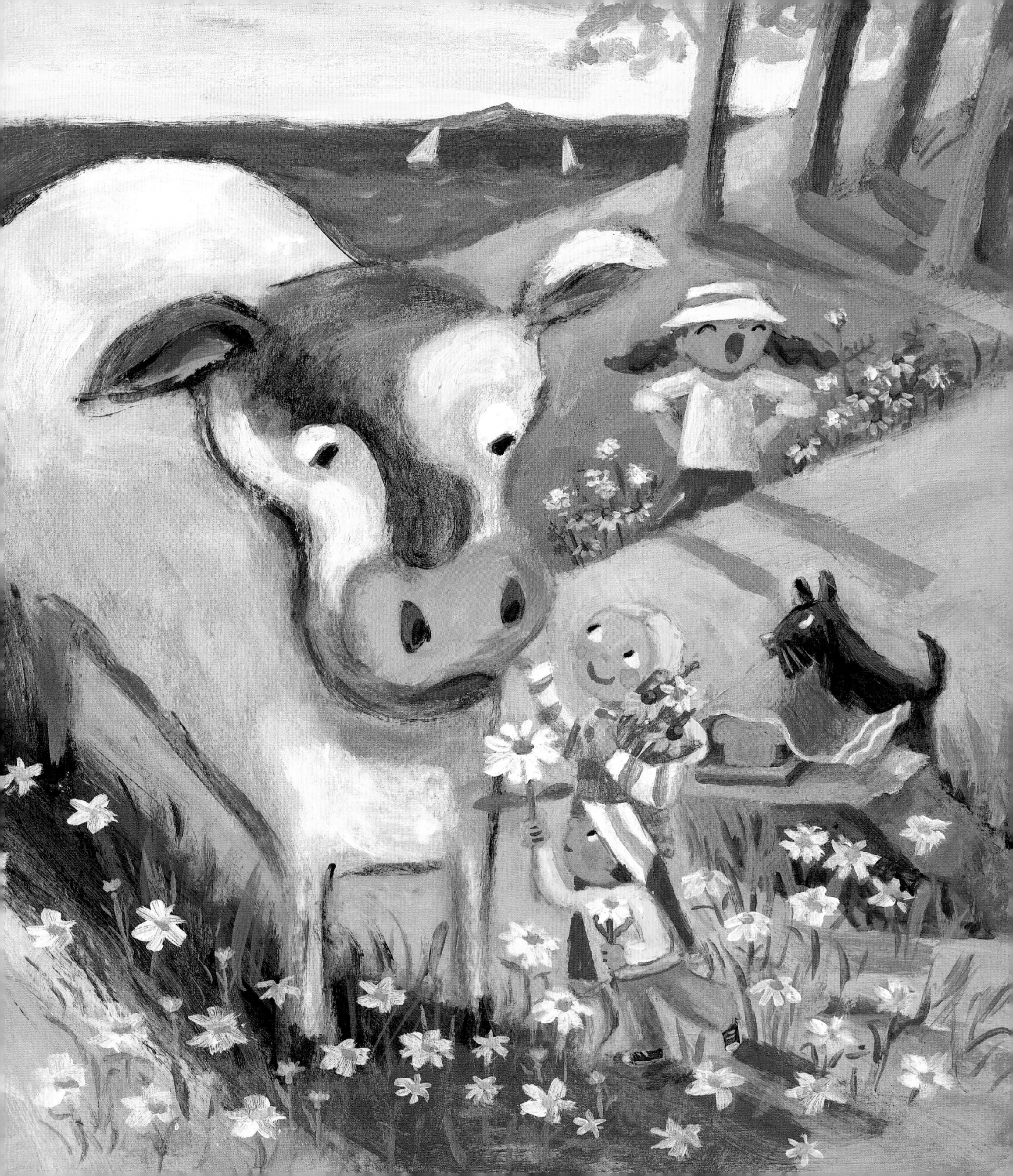

Bless the Island-pastured cow
for her milk which now we pour.

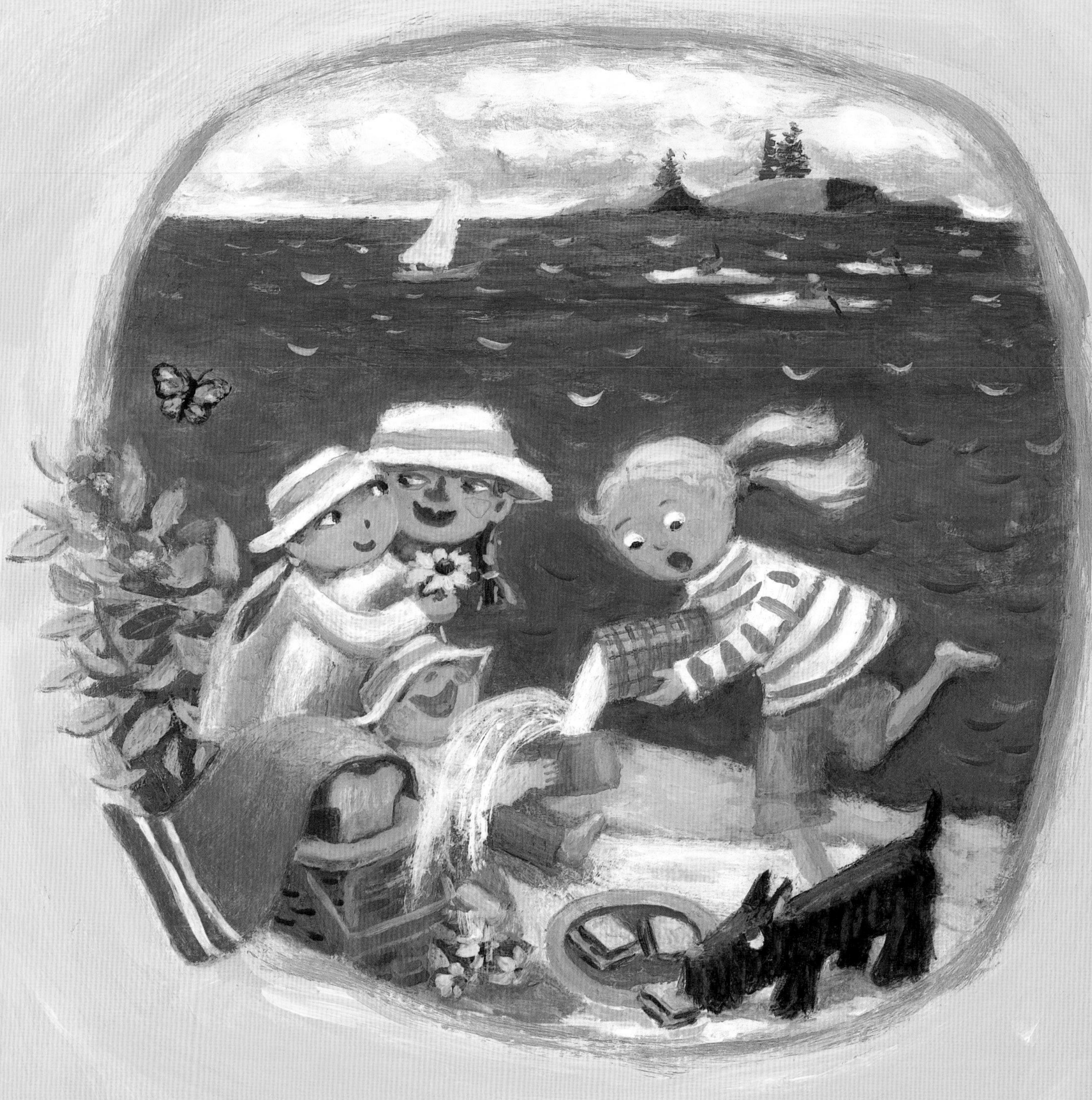

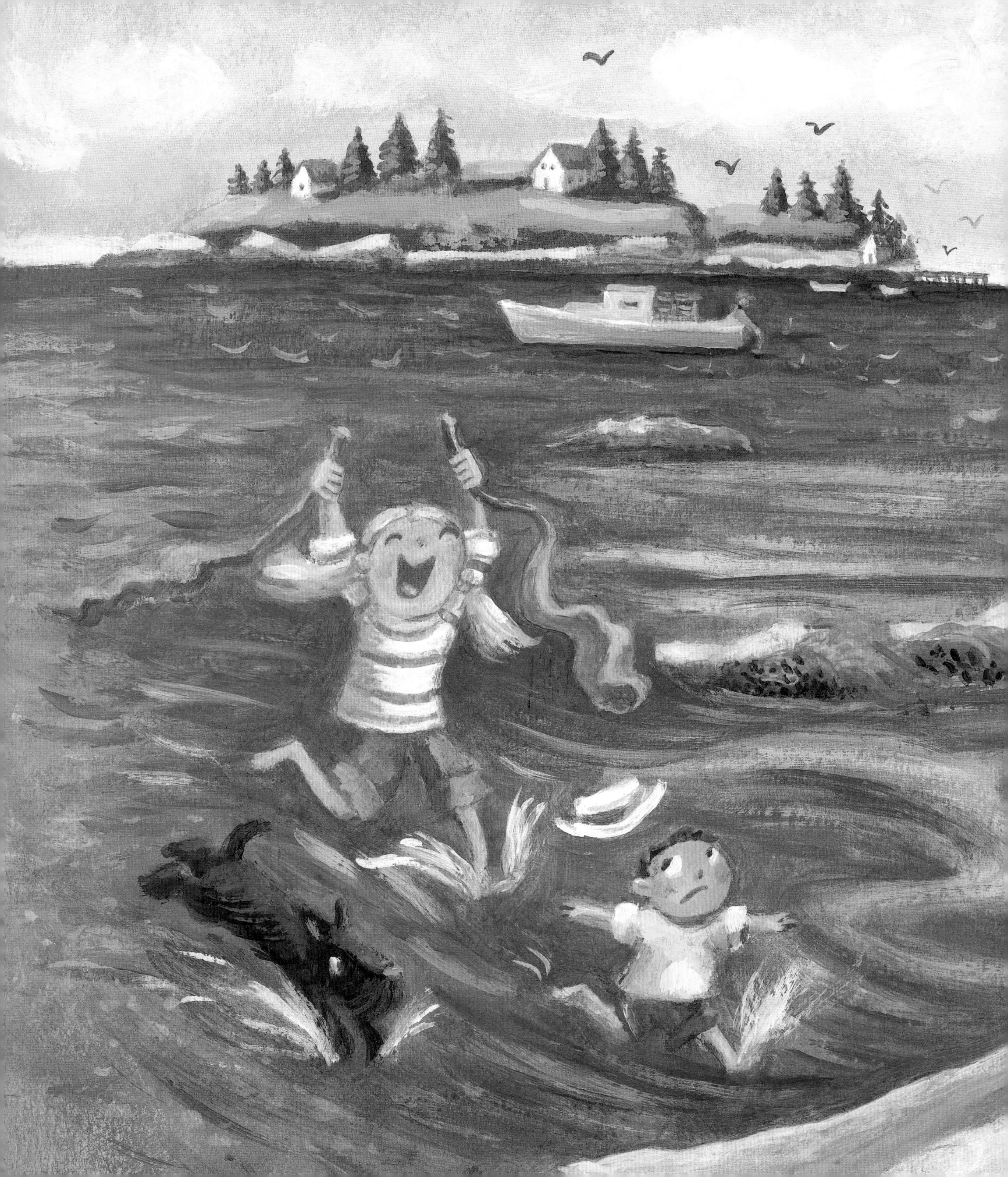

Bless these berries from the shore.

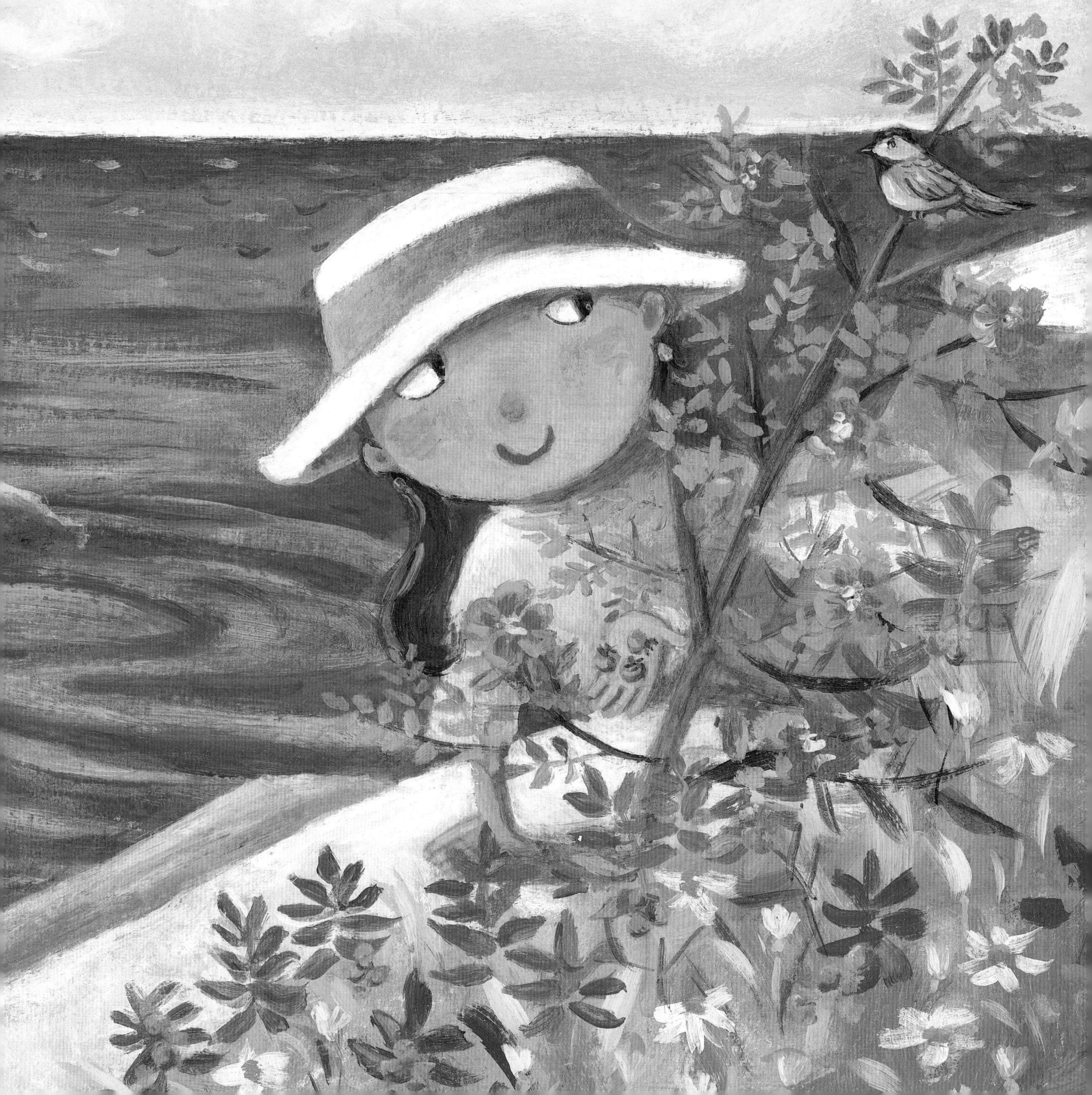

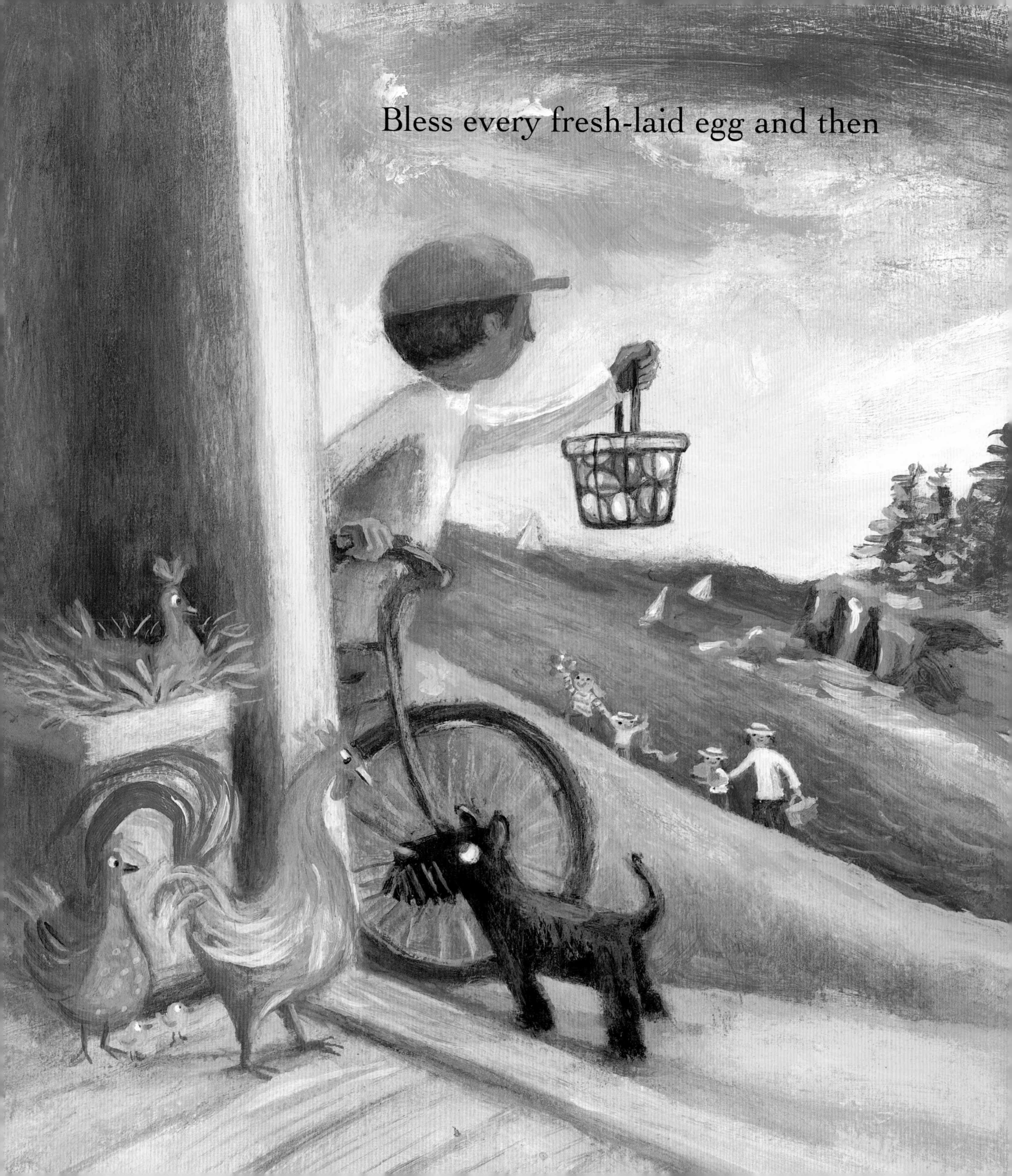

Bless every fresh-laid egg and then

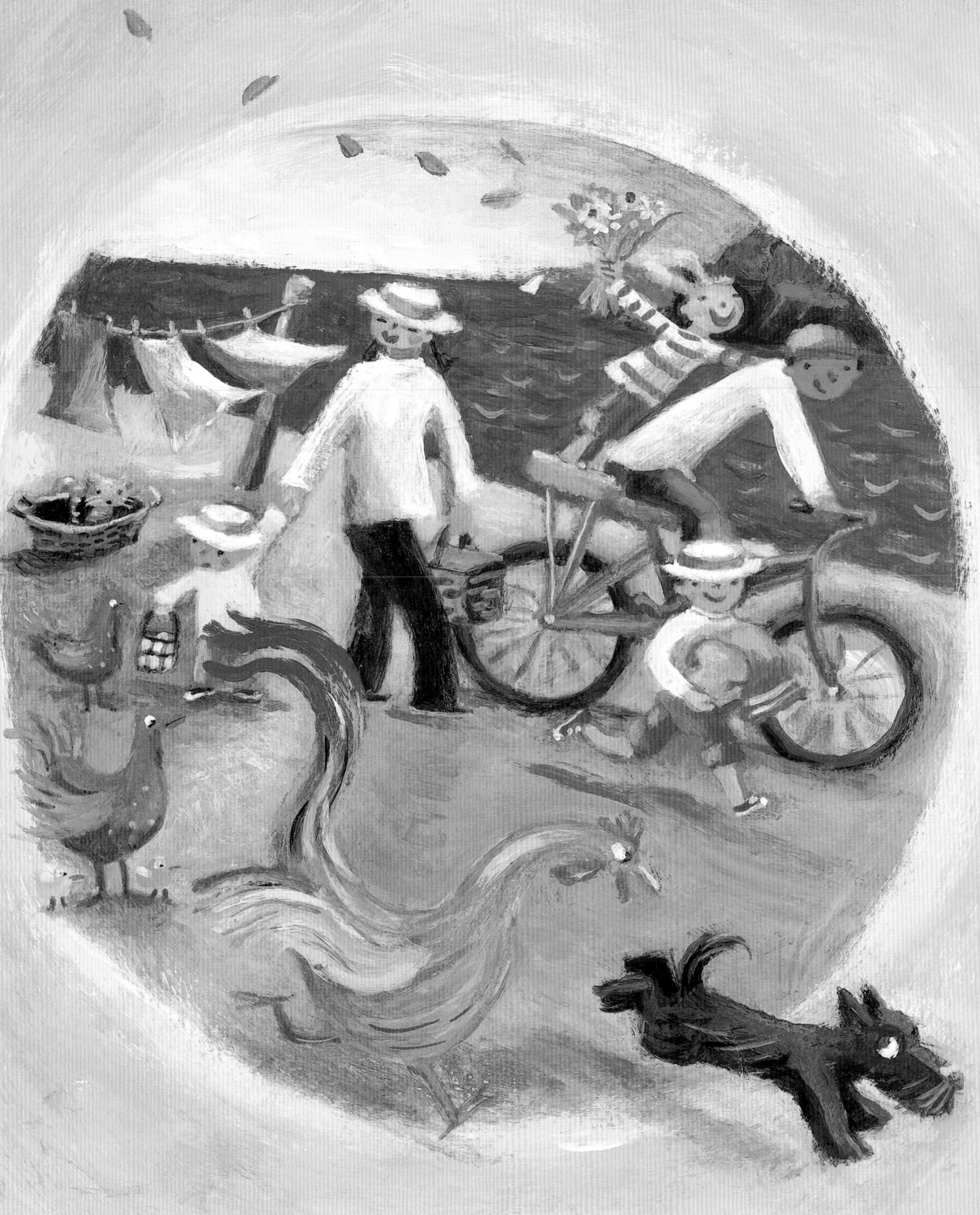

blessings on each Island hen.

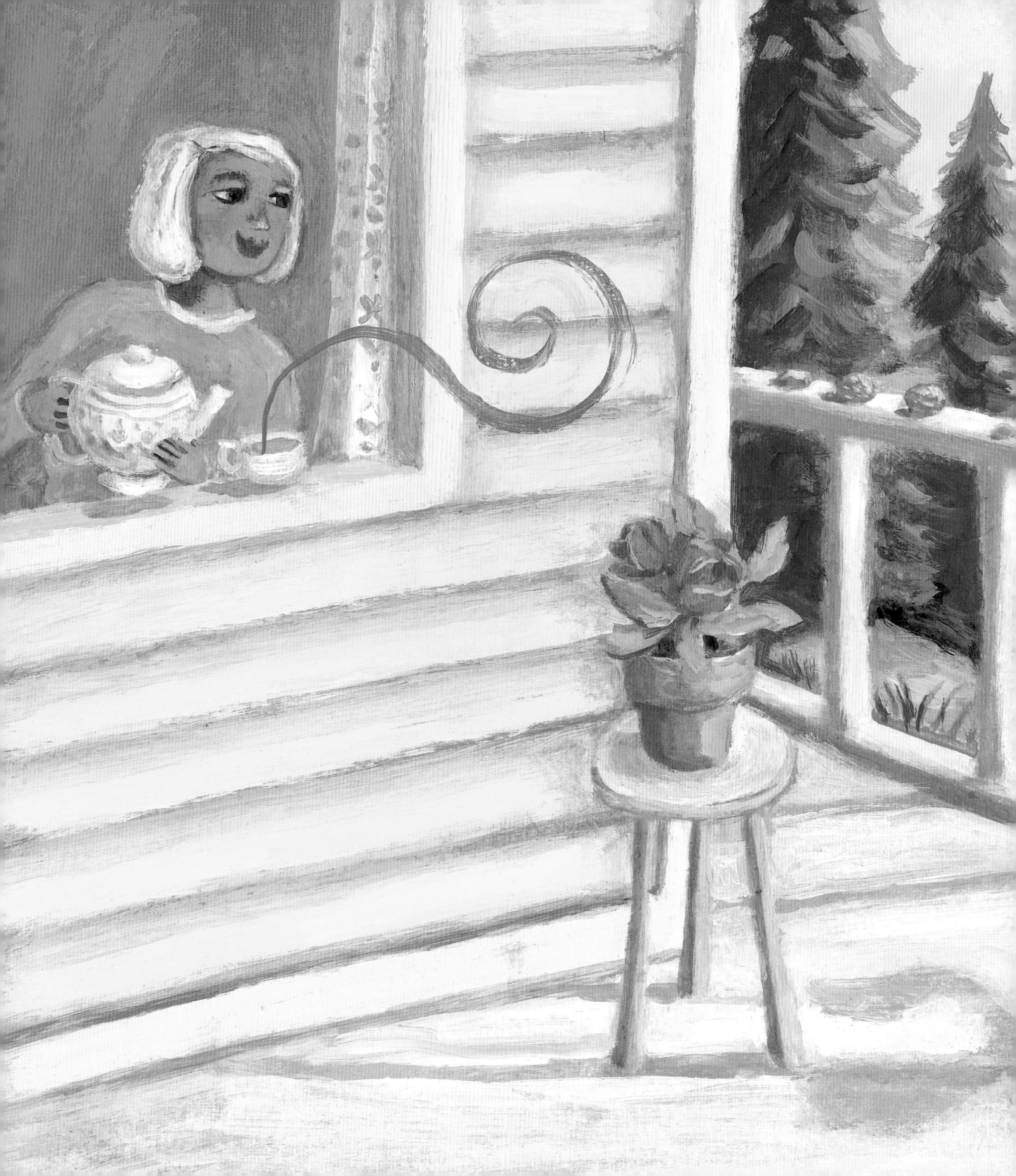

Bless the sweet-smelling bowl of bay;
this tea from islands far away.

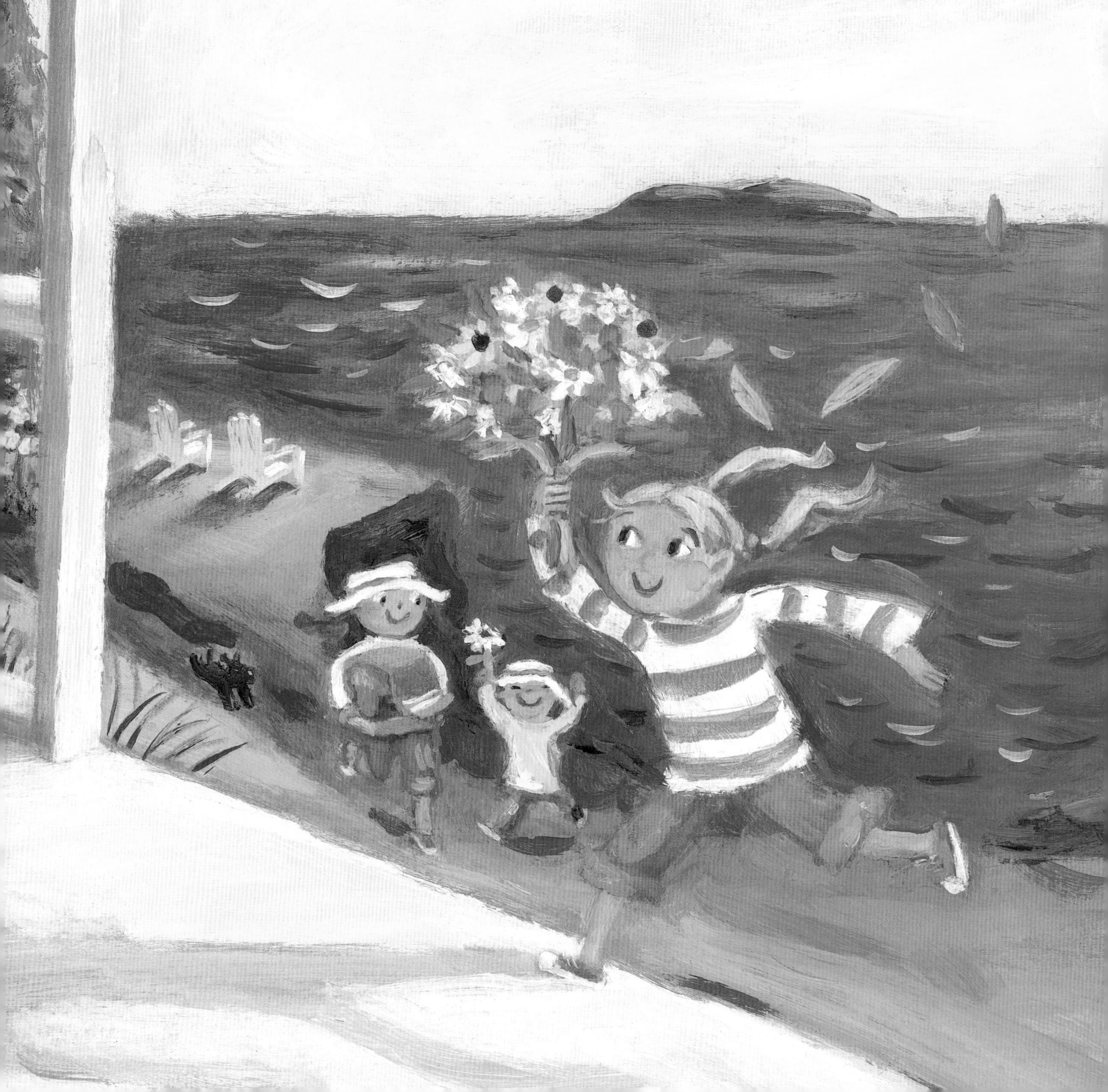

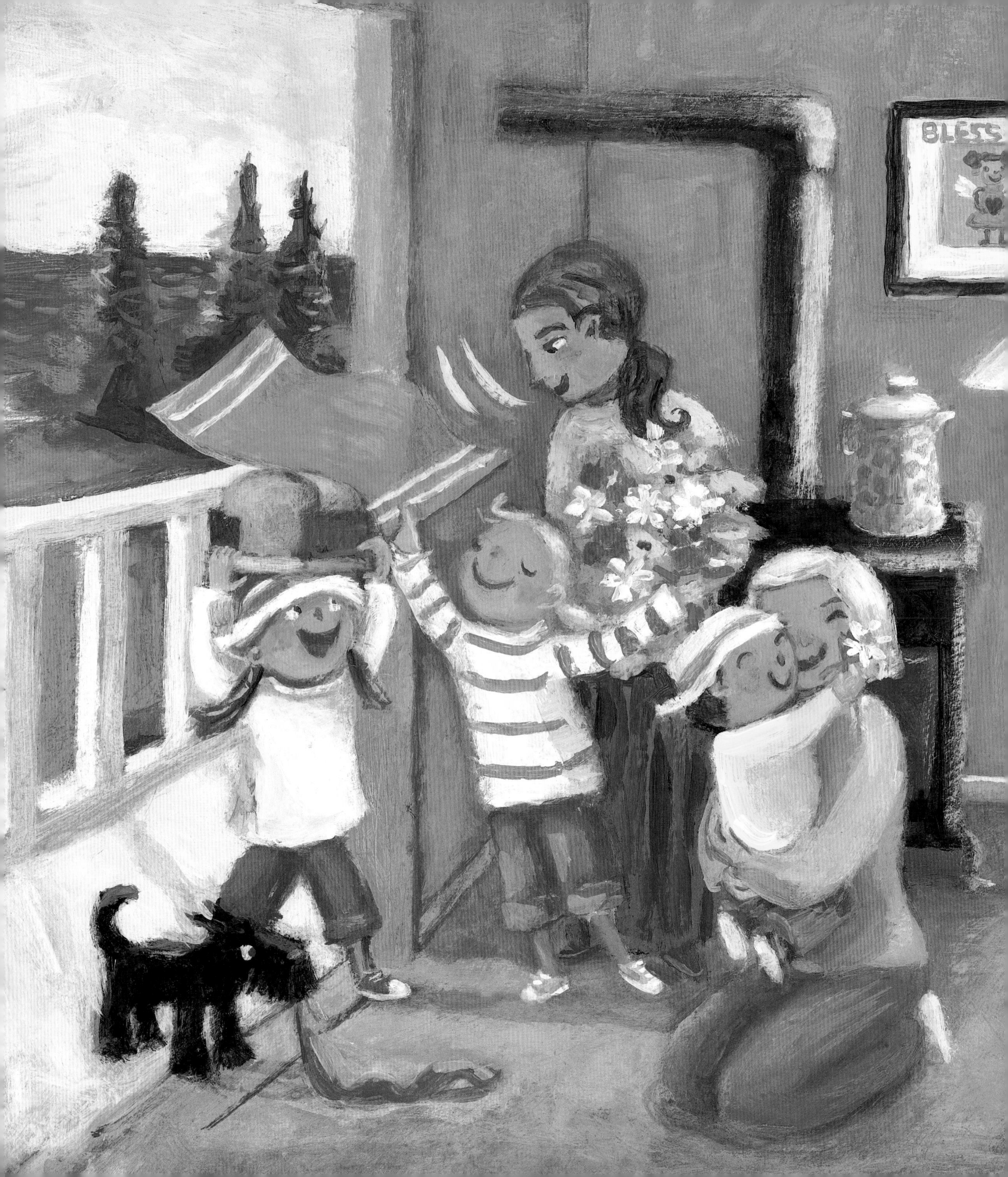
BLESS

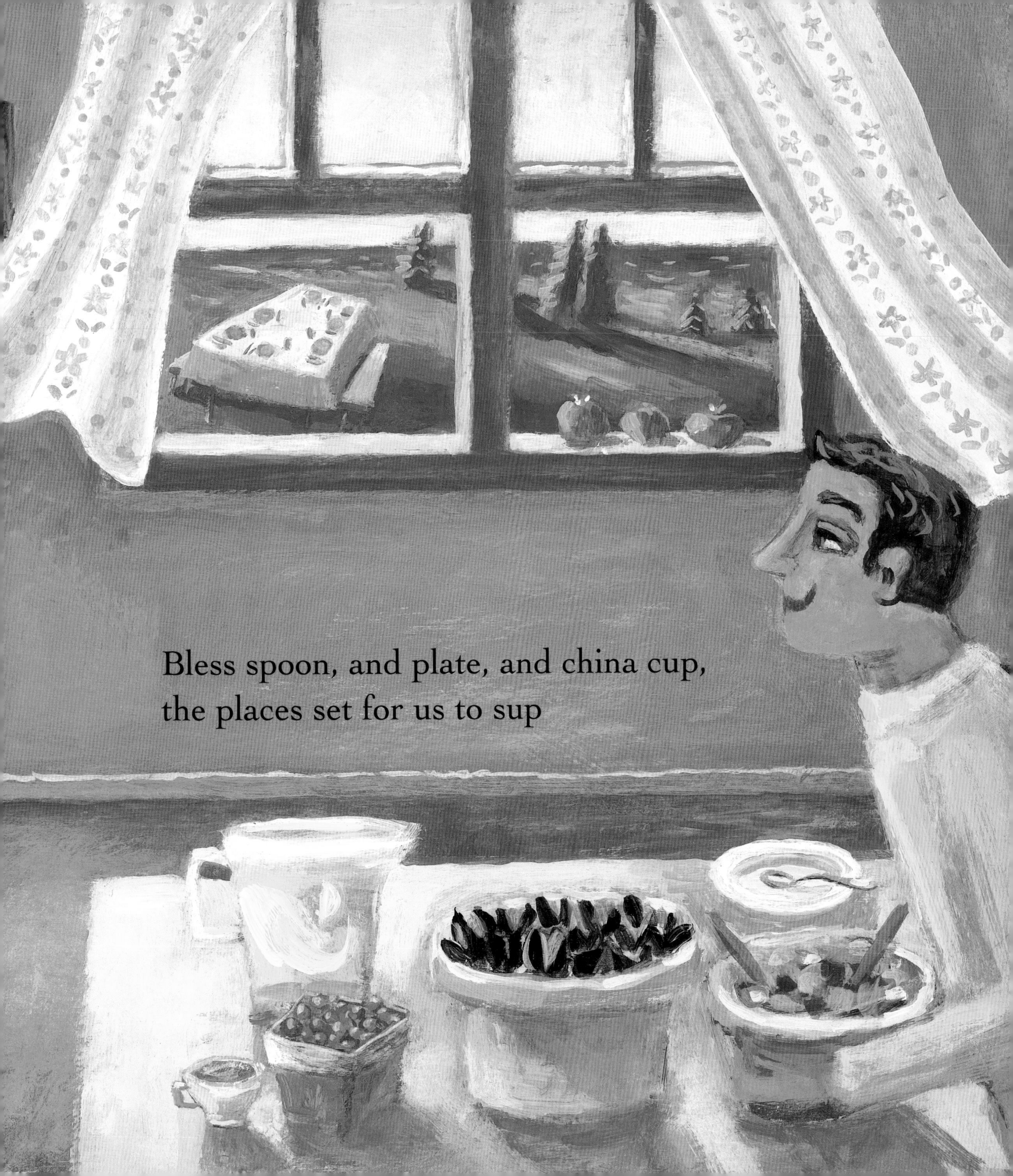

Bless spoon, and plate, and china cup,
the places set for us to sup

in sight of sky, in sound of sea—
Bless old and young,

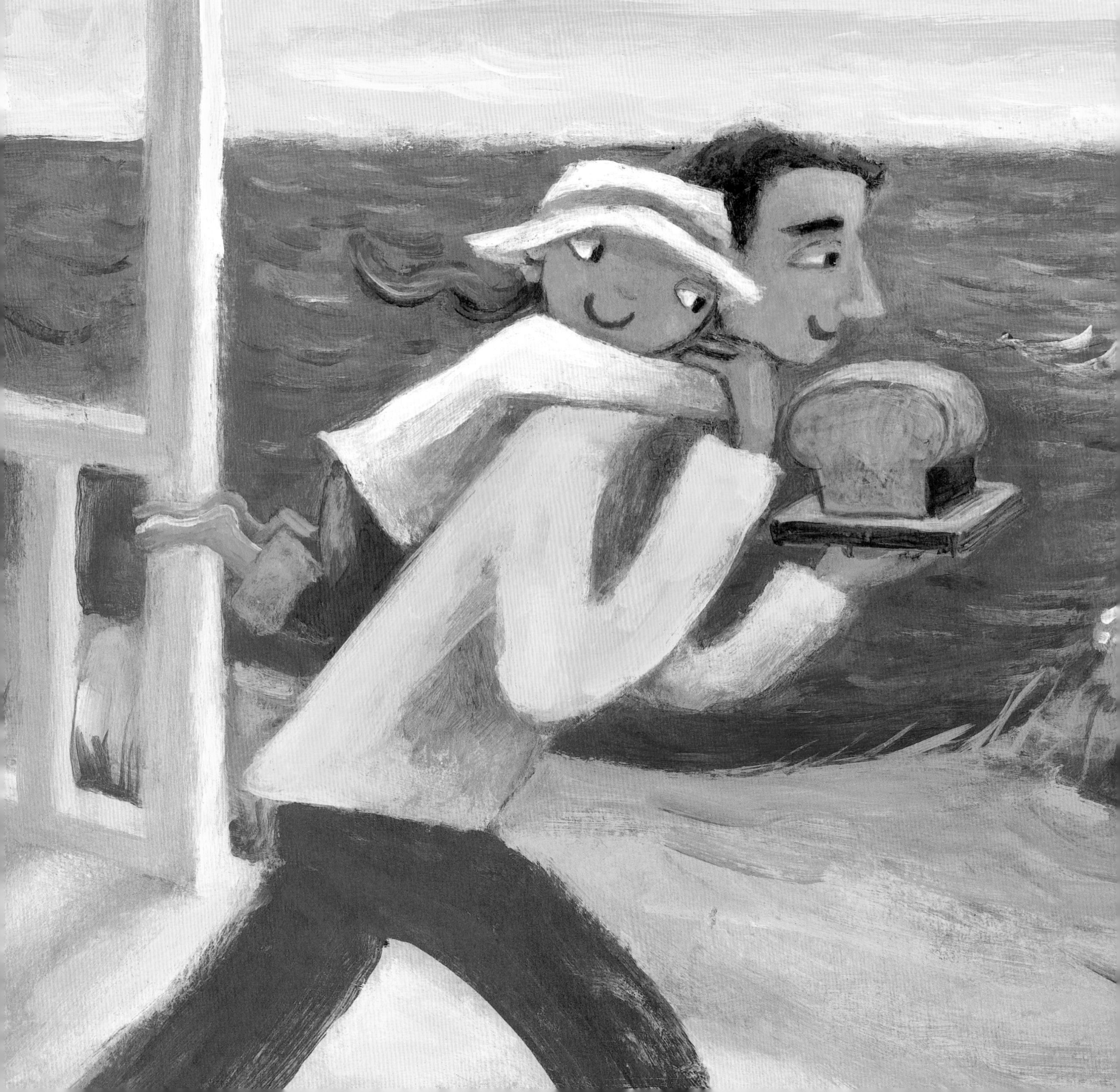

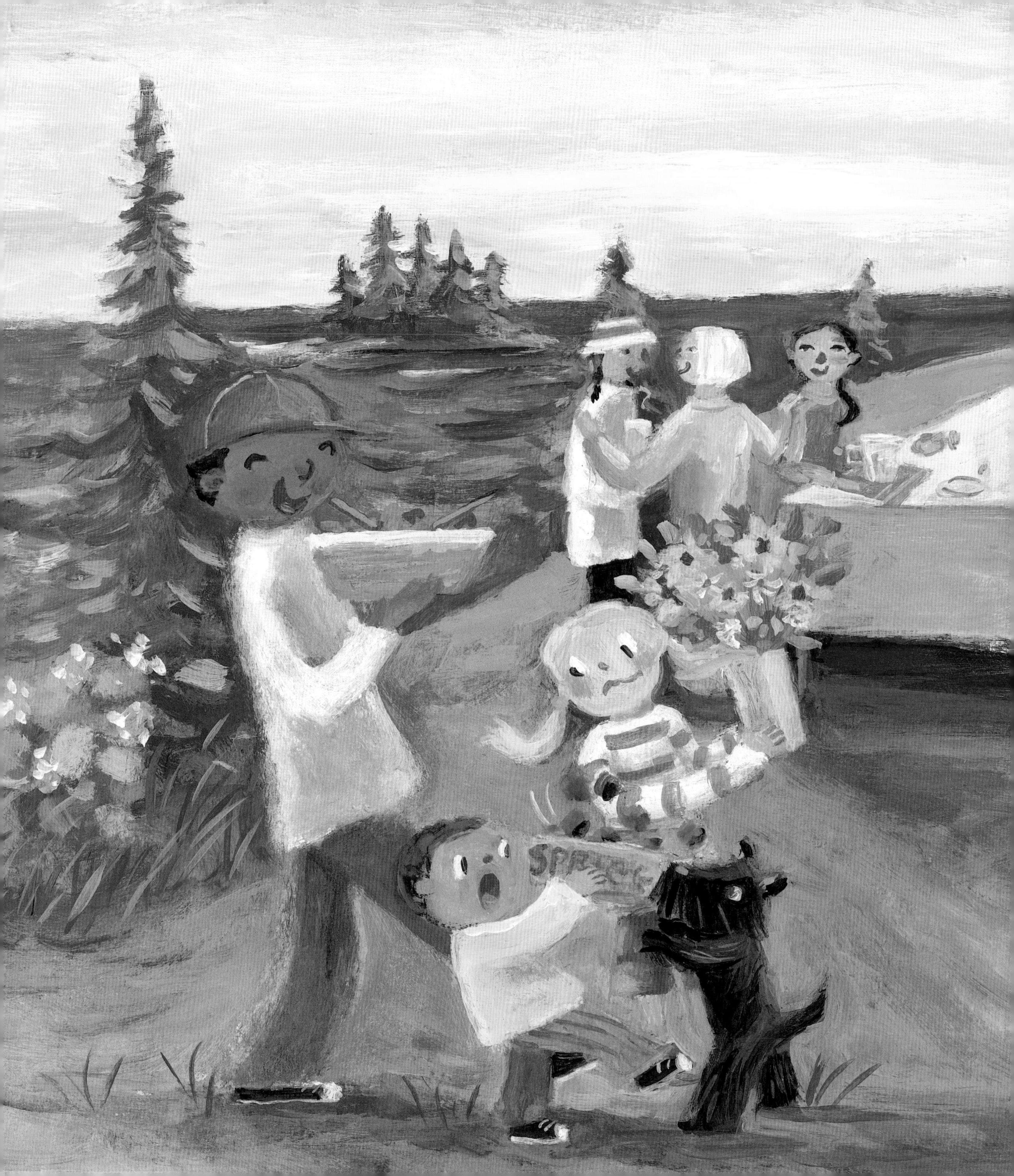

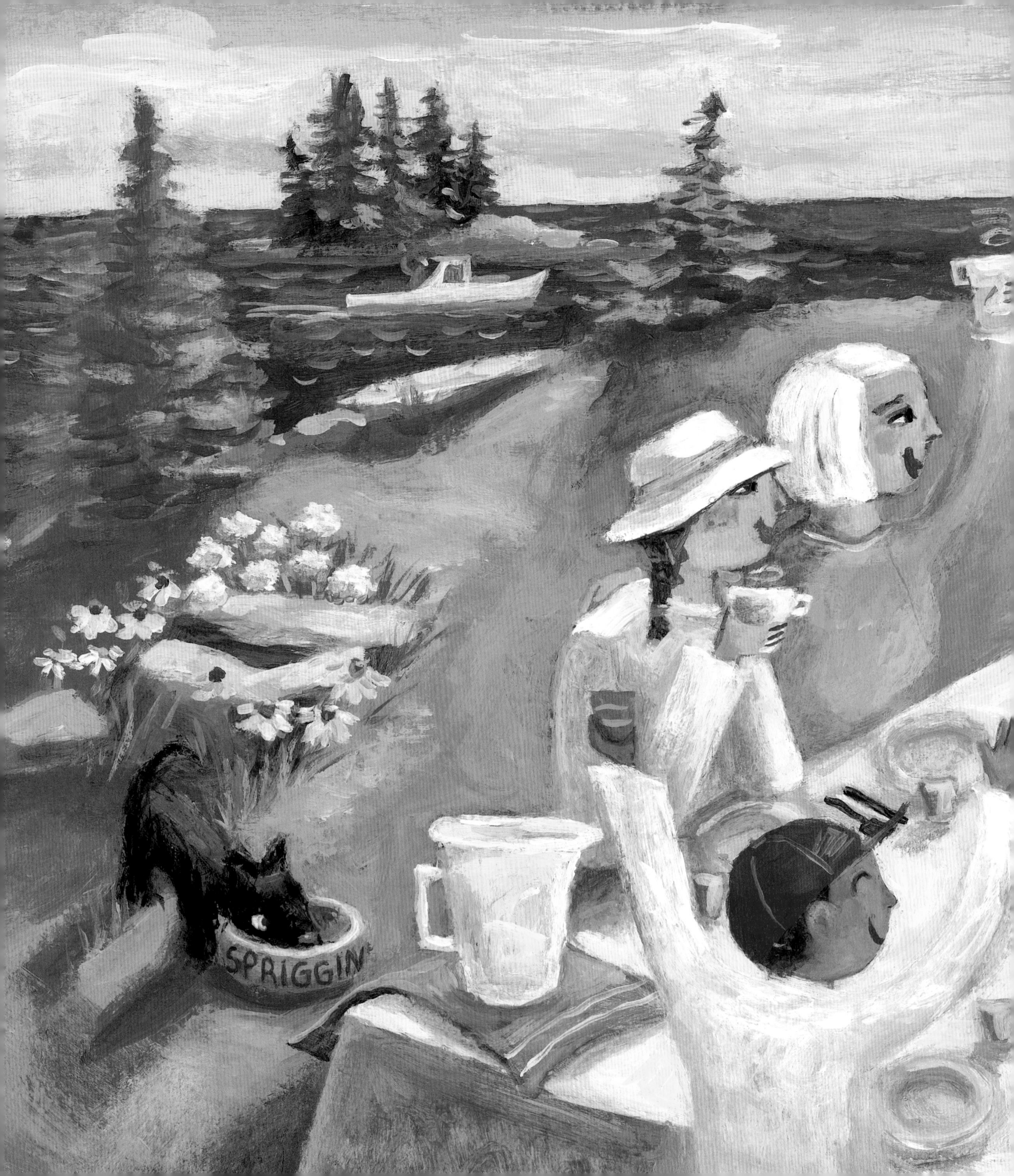
SPRIGGIN

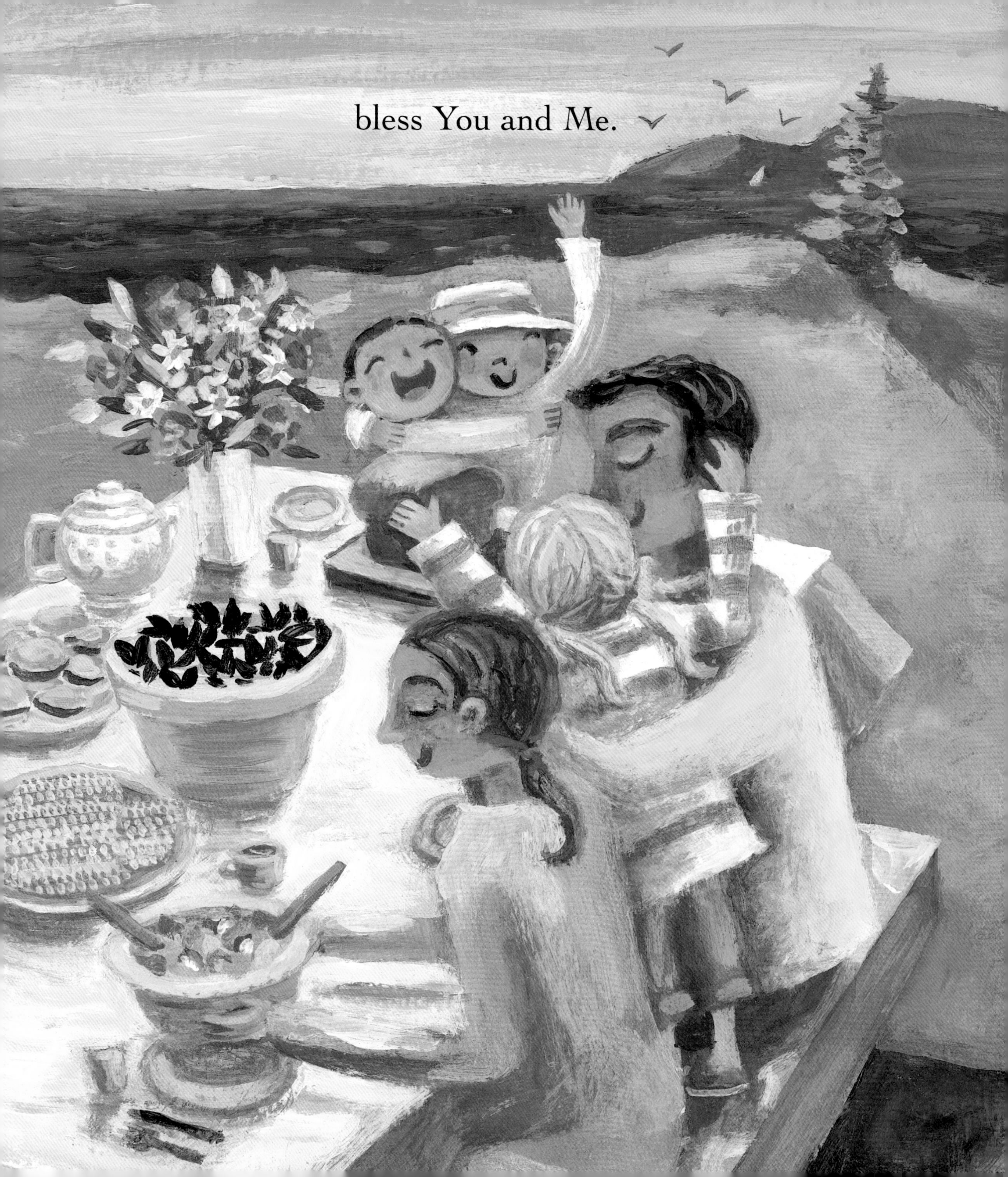

bless You and Me.

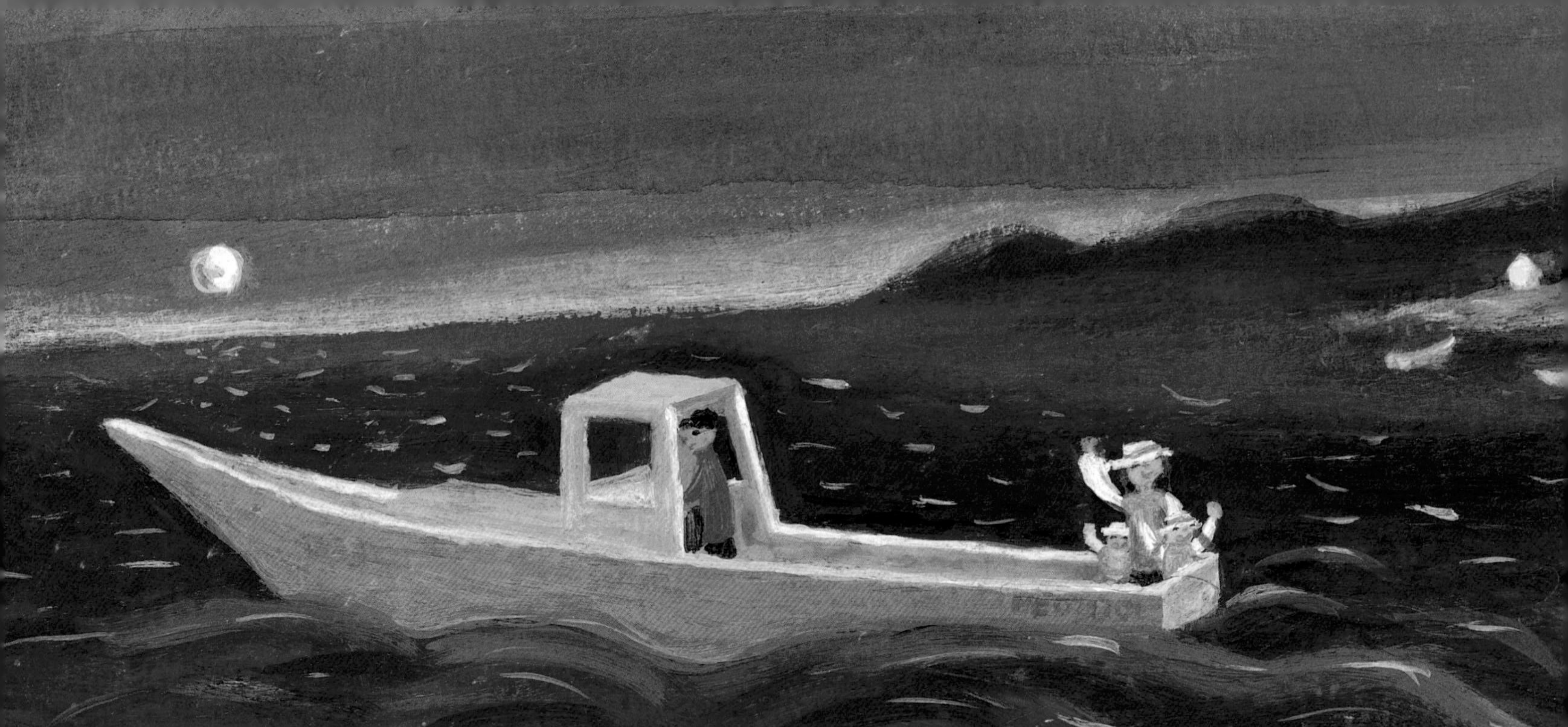

Grace for an Island Meal

Bless this board and bless this bread.
Bless this skylight overhead
through which any eye may see
wheeling gull and blowing tree.
Bless this cloth of woven blue.
Bless these chanterelles that grew
in secret under mossy bough.
Bless the Island-pastured cow
for her milk which now we pour.
Bless these berries from the shore.
Bless every fresh-laid egg and then
blessings on each Island hen.
Bless the sweet-smelling bowl of bay;
this tea from islands far away.
Bless spoon, and plate, and china cup,
the places set for us to sup
in sight of sky, in sound of sea—
Bless old and young, bless You and Me.